The Ghost of Genny Castle

JOHN ESCOTT

Level 2

Series Editors: Andy Hopkins and Jocelyn Potter

Pearson Education Limited
Edinburgh Gate, Harlow,
Essex CM20 2JE, England
and Associated Companies throughout the world.

ISBN: 978-1-4058-6953-9

First published by Penguin Books 1995
Published by Addison Wesley Longman Ltd and Penguin Books Ltd 1998
This edition first published 2008

9 10 8

Text copyright © John Escott 1995
Illustrations copyright © Kay Dixey 1995
This edition copyright © Pearson Education Ltd 2008

The moral right of the author and of the illustrator has been asserted

Typeset by Graphicraft Ltd, Hong Kong
Set in 11/14pt Bembo
Printed in China
SWTC/08

Published by Pearson Education Ltd in association with
Penguin Books Ltd, a Penguin Random House company.

For a complete list of the titles available in the Penguin Readers series please write to your local
Pearson Longman office or to: Penguin Readers Marketing Department, Pearson Education,
Edinburgh Gate, Harlow, Essex CM20 2JE, England.

Contents

Introduction

Claire looked across the fields and saw a tall stone building. 'An old castle!' she said. 'I must go and see that before I go home again.'

Aunt Min didn't look at the castle. 'It — it's not a nice place to visit,' she said. 'Genny Castle is dangerous.'

'Dangerous?' said Claire. 'Why?'

When Claire's mother and father have to go away for a month, Claire stays with her Aunt Min for Christmas. Aunt Min lives in the village of Little Genny, and near it is an old castle. Claire is very interested in the castle, but the people in the village don't want to talk about it. They are afraid of it. Accidents happen there. People die.

Aunt Min tells Claire, 'Stay away from the castle.' But Claire can't stay away. She has to find answers. And she will, because something in the castle is waiting for her . . .

John Escott was born in a small town in the west of England. Now he lives in Bournemouth in the south of England, near the sea. Not far from Bournemouth is an old castle — Corfe Castle. It is nearly one thousand years old, and people tell a lot of stories about it. John wrote *this* story after he visited Corfe Castle.

John writes books for readers of all ages. When he is not writing, he likes walking for hours on quiet beaches, watching films from the 1940s and 1950s, or looking for interesting old books in little bookshops.

His other Penguin Readers and Penguin Active Reading titles are *Hannah and the Hurricane*, *Newspaper Chase*, *The Big Bag Mistake*, *Lucky Break* (all Easystarts), *The Missing Coins* (Level 1), *The Climb* (Level 3) and *Detective Work* (Level 4).

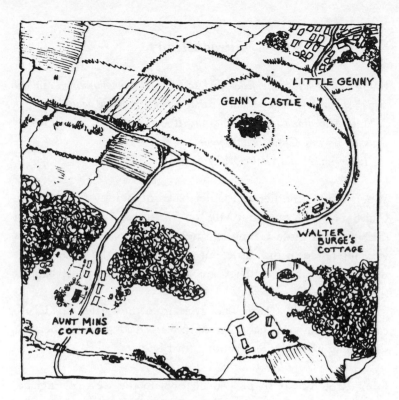

Aunt Min's Cottage, Walter Burge's Cottage,
Genny Castle and Little Genny.

Chapter 1   The Castle

It was a cold December afternoon. Walter Burge was outside his cottage when he saw the car in the road, across the fields. It was Minnie Dawe's car.

'Who's *she* taking home?' thought Walter. 'A visitor?'

Walter didn't like visitors. 'Stay away from the castle,' he told them when they came in the summer. Sometimes they didn't listen to him. But this was winter, when not many people came.

He watched the car for a minute or two, then he went back to his work.

♦

An orange cat was outside the cottage. It was the colour of fire. It too watched the car. Then it walked slowly across the field at the back of the cottage and up to Genny Castle.

♦

Claire looked out of the window of the little car.

'Is it far to your cottage, Aunt Min?' she asked.

'About six miles,' said her aunt.

The village of Little Genny was behind them now, and snow began to fall from the grey December sky. Claire thought about Christmas. 'It's going to be nice here with Aunt Min,' she thought.

'The last time I saw you was ten years ago,' said Aunt Min.

'I was only five years old then,' said Claire with a laugh.

'And now you're as tall as me,' said Aunt Min. She was tall and thin with grey hair. 'Where did your mother and father go? I can't remember.'

'New Zealand,' said Claire. 'They went because of Dad's job, and they're coming back in January.'

Aunt Min smiled. 'And you're going to be with me in my little cottage for Christmas,' she said.

Claire smiled back, then she looked across the fields and saw a tall stone building.

'An old castle!' she said. 'I must go and see that before I go home again.'

Aunt Min didn't look at the castle. 'It – it's not a nice place to visit,' she said. 'Genny Castle is dangerous.'

'Dangerous?' said Claire. 'Why?'

Aunt Min didn't answer. She looked across the field at the old building and said, 'Stones are always falling from the walls and towers.'

Claire looked at her aunt. 'There's something Aunt Min isn't telling me,' she thought. 'What is it? Does the castle have a secret?'

◆

When Claire got up the next morning the sun was in the sky.

'Did you sleep well?' asked Aunt Min.

'Yes, very well,' said Claire.

After breakfast Aunt Min said, 'I must go to the church in Little Genny this morning. Do you want to come with me? You can look round the village.'

'OK,' said Claire.

An hour later they drove to Little Genny. There was some snow on the fields and the castle was beautiful. '*Is* it dangerous?' thought Claire.

Her aunt stopped the car in the village.

'I can walk up to the church and meet you later,' said Claire.

She wanted to get her aunt something for Christmas, and after Aunt Min drove away she went into a small shop. It sold

'An old castle!' Claire said. 'I must go and see that before I go home again.'

books, pictures, writing-paper and envelopes, and a lot of other things.

'Aunt Min likes writing long letters to her friends,' thought Claire. 'I can get her some writing-paper and envelopes.'

She looked at the books. 'Do you have a book about the castle?' she asked the woman in the shop.

'No,' said the woman, 'we don't.'

'Is there a picture of it that –?' Claire began.

'No,' the woman said quickly.

Claire bought a book about old churches, then paid for the writing-paper and envelopes before she went outside.

'What's wrong with Genny Castle?' she thought. 'Nobody likes to talk about it. Why?'

◆

It was good to be out in the sun again, and Claire went for a walk round the village. It was a very pretty place, with a lot of small cottages and a little school. The church was at the top of one of the roads.

Claire was near the church when a big old car stopped in front of her. A man got out. He wore a long, heavy coat and his hair was thick and grey. He carried a shopping-bag in one hand. Some women were outside the shop, but they moved away quickly when they saw the man. He went into the shop.

'Nobody likes Walter Burge,' somebody said.

Claire turned round and saw a boy behind her.

'Why?' she asked.

'I think they're afraid of him,' said the boy. He was about three years younger than Claire. He wore jeans and a warm coat.

'Why?' Claire asked again.

The boy put a finger to his head. 'Crazy,' he said. 'They think old Walter is crazy. Perhaps he is. He lives in the cottage near the castle.'

4

'Do you have a book about the castle?' Claire asked the
woman in the shop.

Some women were outside the shop, but they moved away quickly when they saw Walter.

'What's wrong with the castle?' said Claire.

The boy looked round, but there was nobody listening. 'It's a bad place,' he said. 'Bad things happen there. My dad sometimes talks about it.'

'What *things* happen at the castle?' Claire asked. 'I really want to know.'

'Accidents,' said the boy. 'Some years ago a woman died there. Some of the tall tower – the Black Tower it's called – fell down. She was under it.'

Claire thought for a minute, then she said, 'Accidents can happen. A place isn't *bad* because accidents happen there.'

'*She* does it!' said the boy.

'"She"?' said Claire. 'Who's "she"?'

'The ghost,' the boy said quietly.

'Ghost?' said Claire. She laughed.

'Don't laugh!' said the boy. He was angry. 'People in the village don't talk about it.' And he walked away.

'Ghosts!' Claire thought. She smiled. 'That *boy* is crazy, not the old man. I'm going to see that castle before I go home. But perhaps it's better to say nothing to Aunt Min. I don't want to worry her.'

Claire opened the door of the church and went inside. She saw her aunt and some other women with flowers in their hands. She watched them put the flowers round the building.

Aunt Min saw her. 'We're getting it ready for Christmas Day,' she said.

'The flowers are beautiful,' said Claire.

'There's an evening of Christmas singing here tomorrow,' Aunt Min said, 'for the people in the village.'

'Can we come?' said Claire.

'Do you want to?' said her aunt.

'Yes,' said Claire.

Aunt Min smiled. 'Good, because I do too,' she said. 'Did you have an interesting morning?'

Claire remembered the old man – Walter Burge – and the boy.

'Yes,' she said. 'Very interesting.'

Chapter 2   The Witch Story

After lunch Claire said, 'I'm going for a walk.'

'Don't get lost,' Aunt Min told her.

There was a cold wind, and it got colder when she arrived at the castle field. But it was a nice, sunny afternoon – an afternoon to laugh at stories about ghosts, she thought.

Claire saw the cottage and she saw Walter Burge outside it again. His car was near the cottage. She did not want him to see her, so she moved across and up the field quickly. From time to time she looked back at the cottage. It got smaller and smaller as she got closer to the castle.

Soon she was near the dark towers. There was no sun here and it was very cold. Everything was quiet. There were no sounds of birds or animals.

The cottage was far below her. 'I'm OK now,' she thought. 'He can't see me.'

She went over to the tallest tower – the Black Tower, the boy called it. Did the woman die here? There was a door at the bottom. Inside, stone stairs went up to the top.

Suddenly Claire was afraid. 'Why am I afraid?' she thought. 'Ghosts?'

Then she heard a sound.

She thought it was a bird and looked up quickly...

... *and a big stone fell from the top of the tower.*

Something in her head said *MOVE!* Claire jumped away and

. . . and a big stone fell from the top of the tower.

threw herself down. The big stone hit the bottom stair and broke, and for a minute or two Claire could not move.

Another accident? said something in her head.

She looked up at the top of the tower. Somebody... some*thing* was up there! What was it? It had a head the colour of fire. But was it a man or a woman? Or was it a bird? Claire waited for it to fly down.

And then it was not there.

♦

Walter Burge heard the stone fall and looked up at the castle. His face was white and he was afraid. He saw somebody running down the field.

'Stop!' Walter called. 'Stop!'

But the girl ran on, too fast for Walter's old legs to catch her.

♦

Claire ran back to Aunt Min's cottage.

'Is that you, Claire?' said Aunt Min.

'Yes,' Claire answered. She waited at the back door for a minute before she went into the room at the front of the cottage.

'Claire!' said Aunt Min, looking at her. 'What's wrong? Your shirt is all dirty.'

'I – I fell over,' said Claire. 'Don't worry, I'm OK.' She tried to smile.

'Come and sit down,' said her aunt. 'Let's have a cup of tea.'

Claire sat down in a chair. Then she saw something in the corner of the room. 'You've got a Christmas tree!'

Aunt Min smiled. 'The day after tomorrow is Christmas Day, remember,' she said. 'I brought it in from the garden and put it up when you went for your walk. Do you like it?'

'Yes!' said Claire, laughing now.

'There are some lights to go on it,' said Aunt Min. 'I think

Claire found a very old book. It was small and thin

they're in the little room at the top of the stairs. Perhaps you can look for them in the morning.'

'OK,' said Claire.

♦

Much later, when Claire went to bed, she thought about the castle again.

'I'm not going back,' she thought. 'Genny Castle can have its secrets. I don't want to know them.'

♦

The next morning Claire went up to the little room at the top of the stairs. There were a lot of boxes in the room, two old chairs, a desk with a broken leg and a big cupboard. The Christmas tree lights were in the cupboard. Claire found them easily.

She saw some books at the back of the cupboard. Most of them were stories, but then Claire found a very old book. It was small and thin, and she read the words on the front of it: *The Story of Genny Castle.*

'Did you find the lights, Claire?' Aunt Min called from the bottom of the stairs.

'Yes,' Claire said.

She put the book inside her shirt. 'I don't want Aunt Min to know that I have it,' she thought. 'Why?' But she did not have an answer to her question.

Later that morning she went to her bedroom and began to look at the book. There were pictures of the castle and stories about people. These people lived at the castle many years ago. Some were famous, some were good, and some were bad.

Suddenly Claire saw a word.

Witch.

She began to read.

♦

'She's going to die!' the man said.
'Who can help her?'

A woman came to the castle about two hundred years ago. She was a servant. Where did she come from? Nobody asked her, but soon after she came things began to go wrong. Servants were ill. Animals began to die. Everybody at the castle was afraid. 'What's happening?' they asked.

'It's the new servant!' somebody said. 'She's a witch!'

'A witch, yes!' said the others. 'She must die! Burn her!'

The man living at the castle had a daughter. She was fifteen years old. One day she too was ill.

'She's going to die!' the man said. 'Who can help her?'

'The witch can help her,' his servants told him. And they brought the woman to him.

'Please help my daughter!' the man said to the witch.

'No!' she said. 'It's right for your daughter to die. You burned my sister three years ago!'

'No!' said the man.

'You lived at a different castle then, and my sister and I were two of your servants,' said the woman. 'My sister, Alexa –'

'Alexa!' said the man. 'I remember! I remember her because she was a witch too! She was dangerous, so we burned her. And you are her sister?'

'Yes,' said the witch. 'I watched somebody I loved die. Now you are going to watch your daughter die.'

'No, please!' said the man. 'Help her!'

'Never!' said the witch.

And a week later the girl died.

After that, they took the witch to the top of the Black Tower and burned her.

Today, people say that they see and hear the ghost of the witch on the tower at midnight. They say that they see her fire-coloured hair and her green eyes.

♦

Claire stopped reading. She did not want to know any more.

. . . they took the witch to the top of the Black Tower and burned her.

Chapter 3   An Accident in the Snow

Claire and her aunt drove to the church that evening. There was a strong wind and snow started to fall again. Claire watched it through the car window. But she did not think about the snow or about Christmas: she thought about the witch and about the fire-coloured *thing* that she saw on the top of the Black Tower after the stone fell. These thoughts stayed with her all evening and she only half-listened to the singing in the church. She could not get the story of the witch out of her head.

When the Christmas singing was finished, she and Aunt Min went back to the car through the snow. Now it came up over their shoes, and the night was very cold.

The car made lines in the snow when they drove away from the church, and everything was white – white houses, white trees, white cars, people's white coats. Soon they were in the little roads outside the village and there were no other cars, only Aunt Min's. Driving was difficult. The car could not stop easily in the snow. Aunt Min drove carefully, but with a worried face.

They were in the road near the castle. Aunt Min tried to drive slowly – but the car went faster and faster in the snow!

'I can't stop it!' she said.

And then the car went off the road and hit a tree!

Aunt Min put her hands to her face and shut her eyes.

'Are you OK?' Claire asked.

'Y-yes, I think so,' said her aunt.

They got out of the car and looked at it.

'I can't drive it now,' said Aunt Min. 'I must phone the garage in the village. Mr Perkins can drive out and see it tomorrow. But now we must get home, Claire.'

Claire looked across the fields. She could see Genny Castle. Aunt Min looked at the castle too and Claire could read her

And then the car went off the road and hit a tree!

aunt's thoughts: it was more than two miles round the road, but it was not a mile across the fields.

'Let's go across Walter Burge's field,' said Aunt Min. 'I can't walk all round the road.'

She got a light from inside the car, then they went into the field and began to walk through the snow.

Claire tried not to look at the castle.

◆

Walter Burge sat in a big chair in front of the fire in his cottage. There was a book about castles in his hands. There were other books in the little room and many of them were about castles too.

His cat, Alexa, sat by the fire.

Walter knew the stories that people in the village told about him. 'He's crazy,' they said, and he knew this. And he knew the stories about the castle. People said it was a bad, dangerous place. He didn't try to stop these stories, because people stayed away when they heard them, and Walter didn't want people to go near the castle. He knew that the castle had its secrets.

He stopped reading and closed his eyes.

Alexa, the cat, stood up. She walked into the kitchen without making a sound, and across to a window. The window was not quite shut and she pushed it with her foot. When it was open, Alexa jumped down into the snow.

She began to walk up to the castle.

◆

Walter opened his eyes. 'It's time I went to bed, Alexa,' he said.

Then he saw that the cat was not there, and he got up out of the chair and walked through to the kitchen.

'Alexa?' he said. He saw the open window. 'Again?' he said. 'Why did you go out on a night like this?'

18

When the window was open, Alexa jumped down into the snow.

Walter knew that the cat went up to the castle. He remembered other nights – nights when people in the village heard sounds and saw lights on the Black Tower. Nights when Walter shut his cottage doors and stayed inside.

Walter tried not to think about these things. He loved his castle, but he knew that the village people were worried about it. 'The castle is a bad place,' they said. 'Pull it down!' Walter did not want that to happen.

'I must stop you, Alexa,' he said.

And he took a light from a cupboard, pulled on his shoes and coat, and went out of the back door, into the snow and the wind.

◆

'I'm so cold,' Claire thought.

She and Aunt Min walked across the field. They could see Walter Burge's cottage, half a mile away. Claire was worried about her aunt. How far could she walk in the snow? The old woman's face was grey and she was very, very tired.

Claire took the light from Aunt Min, then put a hand under her aunt's arm. She helped her across the field to Walter Burge's cottage.

'We must stop here for you to sit down, Aunt Min,' Claire said above the sound of the wind.

Her aunt was too tired to say anything.

The front door of the cottage was shut, but Claire hit it with her hand. 'Mr Burge!' she called. There was no answer. She tried to open the door, but it stayed shut. 'Let's go round to the back,' she told her aunt.

They went round to the back door of the cottage. Claire looked at the snow by the door. 'He's gone out,' she thought. 'I can see his footprints in the snow; they're going up to the castle. But what is he doing up there?'

*Claire took the light from Aunt Min, then put a hand under
her aunt's arm.*

There was no time to think about this – her aunt was cold and tired. Claire pushed open the back door of the cottage and they went inside.

They found the room with the fire and Aunt Min sat on the chair in front of it. Claire went to the kitchen and made her a cup of tea. When she came back Aunt Min's eyes were closed. Claire looked at her watch. The time was eleven o'clock.

After two or three minutes Aunt Min opened her eyes.

'Here's some tea for you,' Claire said.

'Thank you, Claire,' said Aunt Min. Her voice was weak. 'I'm a little better now.'

'You can't walk any more tonight,' said Claire.

'No, I don't think I can,' said her aunt.

'I'm going to find Mr Burge,' said Claire. 'Perhaps he can take us home in his car.'

Aunt Min looked worried. 'Where is he?' she asked.

'I think he's up at the castle,' said Claire.

'Claire, you can't –!' Aunt Min began to say.

'I know about the castle, Aunt Min,' said Claire. 'I'm not afraid.'

But she *was* afraid.

Chapter 4   The Black Tower

Walter Burge looked up at the Black Tower and thought he saw a light; but perhaps he didn't.

'I didn't see it,' he said.

He was afraid, and he knew it. He never went up to the castle at night. He never followed Alexa when she went out. He did not want to see or know the things that happened.

But things *did* happen, because Alexa was *more than a cat*.

Walter Burge looked up at the Black Tower and thought he
saw a light; but perhaps he didn't.

Walter knew the story of Alexa, the witch with the fire-coloured hair. He knew it well. He read it when he was a boy. Then, ten years ago, the cat arrived at his cottage. Walter tried to send it away, but it came back again and again, and every time it came it went up to the castle. After some time Walter stopped trying to send the cat away. He gave it some food and called it Alexa because of its colour. After that, the cat made its home in Walter's cottage.

And then things began to happen.

Birds in the castle began to die. Somebody found a dead dog in one of the towers. A stone from the Black Tower fell on to a woman's head and killed her. A small boy from the village got lost in the castle and his father did not find him for three hours; after that day the boy never spoke again. Then people began to see lights and things moving up on the towers, but when they went to look, there was nothing there. Now the village people stayed away. And nobody ever went up to the castle at night.

Only Alexa.

But tonight Walter was there too. 'Alexa!' he called. 'Alexa!'

The wind took his words and carried them away.

◆

The orange cat sat on the tower. It saw the old man with the light in his hand. Then, far away, it saw another thing moving across the snow. *It was the girl!*

The cat was afraid of the girl. It watched her with its green eyes. Why did the girl come to the castle? What did she want?

◆

Claire followed Walter Burge's footprints in the snow.

24

The cat was afraid of the girl. It watched her with its green eyes.

'They're going up to the Black Tower,' she thought. 'But why?' And who went there before him?' She could see smaller footprints next to Walter's. 'Are they the footprints of a cat?'

She got to the bottom of the Black Tower and stopped. 'Mr Burge!' she called. But the wind was too strong for him to hear her.

'I could wait for him to come down,' she thought. But she remembered her aunt's tired face. 'No, Aunt Min must get home, so I must go and find him.'

The stairs were wet and difficult to see, and the wind was cold and strong. There was nothing to help her up the stairs, and her shoes were heavy with snow.

And then she saw the orange light at the top of the tower. Suddenly there was another sound, above the sound of the wind. What was it? Then she knew.

It was the sound of a fire, of burning.

Claire was very afraid. 'Go back down,' she told herself. 'Now!' But her feet didn't move.

Where was Walter Burge? Was he up there? His footprints went into the tower, but they did not come out again.

'Perhaps he's ill,' thought Claire. 'Perhaps he wants some help.' 'Mr Burge!' she called. 'Mr Burge!'

◆

Walter was inside a big orange light. He could not see through it. There was a fire, and he was in it, but he did not burn.

'Crazy!' he thought.

It was difficult to see in that light, but he could hear the sound. *Aaaaaagh!* The sound was outside his head and inside it at the same time.

'Alexa!' he called. 'Alexa! Stop! Stop this!'

Now he could hear another sound. Weaker. Quieter. What was it? A girl?

26

Walter was inside a big orange light.

'*Mr Burge . . . Mr Burge.*'

'Who is it?' he said. 'What's happening?'

'*It's Claire,*' the girl called.

'Claire? I don't know anybody called Claire,' he said. It was suddenly difficult to stand up. He put a hand on the tower wall.

Claire? *Claire?* He *did* know a Claire. Now who –?

And then he remembered! Claire was the name of the girl – the daughter of the man two hundred years ago at the castle. And she died because the witch did not help her. *Her* name was Claire. He remembered reading it in a book at the cottage.

'Claire?' he said. 'You're Claire? But Claire is dead.'

Some other thing said the name now. '*Claire . . . ?*' Something near him. A woman? He could hear it. He could hear the name in the sound of the fire.

'*Claire? . . . Claire? . . . Claire?*'

The thing sounded very, very afraid.

'*Not dead? . . . Claire? . . . Not dead?*'

Suddenly the fire began to die and the orange light began to go out. Now Walter could see the sky above him and the tower round him.

'*Not dead? . . . Claire? . . . Not . . . ?*'

Slowly the words died too.

Soon there was no fire, no sound. Only the light in Walter's hand.

◆

Claire went up the last of the stairs and out on to the top of the tower. She saw Walter Burge, but he did not hear her. He looked across the fields.

The orange-coloured cat sat on the wall of the tower. It saw Claire . . . *and its eyes were afraid.* It moved away from her.

Walter saw Claire's light. He turned quickly. Claire saw the stones behind him move.

'The wall!' she called.

Walter jumped away from the wall. His light fell from his hand and went out. The stones behind him fell into the night. Then half of the tower began to follow them.

Claire and Walter ran across to the stairs and down them. They looked back when they got to the bottom, when the sound of the falling stones stopped. Most of the Black Tower was suddenly not there.

They looked at it without speaking. Then Walter Burge said, 'We're lucky that we're not dead.'

'Yes,' said Claire. 'But . . . what happened to your cat?'

They found it in the snow at the bottom of the tower. It was dead.

Walter said nothing. He walked away sadly.

◆

Aunt Min opened her eyes when she heard them coming. Mr Burge came in first, then Claire.

'Mr Burge,' Aunt Min began. 'I . . . we –'

'The girl told me about the accident with the car,' said Walter.

Aunt Min looked at Claire. 'Are you all right?'

'Yes,' said Claire. Her face was white.

'Some of the tower fell down,' said Walter. 'The snow . . . it's very heavy . . .' He stopped.

Aunt Min looked at him, then looked back at Claire. 'I think I understand,' she said. And they knew that she did.

'I can take you home in my car,' said Walter.

'Thank you, Mr Burge,' said Aunt Min.

They went outside to Walter's car. The snow stopped falling when they opened the door.

The castle was different. Claire was not afraid of it now.

They sat in the back and Claire looked out of the window at the castle. It was different. She was not afraid of it now. The Black Tower wasn't tall now. Most of it was not there.

Claire looked at her watch; it was after midnight. 'It's Christmas Day,' she said. 'Happy Christmas, Aunt Min. Happy Christmas, Mr Burge.'

'Happy Christmas,' they said together.

◆

Walter walked up to the castle the next morning. He went to the bottom of the Black Tower and looked at the stones.

The fire-coloured cat was not there. He looked for it carefully, but it was not there.

And nobody ever saw the ghost of Genny Castle again.

ACTIVITIES

Chapter 1

Before you read

1 Look at the Word List at the back of the book. Answer these questions with words from the Word List.

   a It has thick, high walls and a tower. What is it?

   b These are small houses. What are they called?

   c Walls are often made of these. What are they?

   d You don't tell other people this. What is it?

   e These people work for rich people. Who are they?

   f Your feet leave these behind in the snow. What are they?

2 Put these words from the Word List into new sentences.

   ago   burn   crazy   far   ghost   must   soon   worry

3 Read the Introduction and the first page of Chapter 1. Answer these questions.

   a What time of the year is it?

   b Who is Minnie Dawe?

   c What is the name of the village?

4 Look at the map opposite page 1. Can you find:

   a Genny Castle?

   b Walter Burge's cottage?

While you read

5 Find the answer to these questions.

   a What is outside Walter Burge's cottage? ....

   b How long ago did Claire see Aunt Min? ....

   c Where in the village does Aunt Min go? ....

   d What does Claire buy for Aunt Min for Christmas? ....

   e What is the name of the tall tower? ....

   f The boy says, '*She* does it!'. Who or what is 'she'? ....

After you read

6 Who says or thinks these words? Who or what are they talking or thinking about?

    a 'Who's *she* taking home?'

    b 'And now you're as tall as me.'

    c 'Nobody likes to talk about it. Why?'

    d 'They think old Walter is crazy.'

7 Work with another student.

    Student A: You are the woman in the shop. Tell your husband about your conversation with Claire (You don't know her name). You're afraid that she'll try to visit the castle.

    Student B: You know the woman in the shop. Ask about the girl. Why is she in the village? Who is she staying with?

Chapter 2

Before you read

8 Look at the name of the chapter. What books or stories do you know about witches? Talk about it with a friend.

9 In this chapter, do you think Claire is going to learn:

    a something about the future?

    b something from a long time ago?

While you read

10 What happens first? What happens next? Write the numbers 1–5.

    a A big stone falls from the top of the Black Tower.   ......

    b Claire sees Walter Burge outside his cottage.   ......

    c Claire tells Aunt Min, 'I fell over.'   ......

    d Claire goes to the Black Tower.   ......

    e Walter runs after Claire but he can't catch her.   ......

11 Are these sentences right (✓) or wrong (✗)?

    a Claire looks for a Christmas tree in the little room.   ......

    b Claire finds a book about Genny Castle.   ......

    c Claire tells Aunt Min about the book.   ......

    d Claire reads about people from two hundred years ago.   ......

    e People now say they see a ghost on the tower.   ......

After you read

12 What do you know about these people?

    a the man and his daughter   **b** Alexa   **c** Alexa's sister

Chapter 3

Before you read

13 Look at the pictures in this chapter. What do you think happens next in the story?

While you read

14 Who says or thinks these words?

    a 'Let's go across Walter Burge's field.'   ....

    b 'Why did you go out on a night like this?'   ....

    c 'We must stop here for you to sit down.'   ....

    d 'I can see his footprints in the snow.'   ....

After you read

15 Answer these questions.

    a Why do Claire and Aunt Min go the church?

    b Why do Claire and Aunt Min walk across Walter Burge's field and not on the road?

    c Where does Alexa go?

    d Why does Walter Burge go up to the castle?

Chapter 4

Before you read

16 What do you think Claire will find at the castle?

17 Is Alexa *only* a cat? What do you think?

While you read

18 Write a word in each sentence.

    a Walter Burge thinks that he sees a .... on the Black Tower.

    b When birds go to the castle, they ....

    c Walter can't hear Claire's call because the .... is very strong.

d Claire sees a light and hears the sound of a ....

e .... is the name of the dead girl from two hundred years ago.

After you read

19 Walter hears these words in the sound of the fire:
'*Claire? .... Claire? .... Not Dead?*' Who can he hear?

20 Use one of these words in each question. Then answer the questions:

Why   What   Who   When

a ... drove the car into the tree?

b ... fell from the Black Tower on to a woman's head?

c ... did the cat first arrive at Walter's cottage?

d ... did Walter go back to the castle the next morning?

Writing

21 You are Claire. Write a letter to your parents. Tell them about the castle.

22 People say there are witches in the world today. Are they right or wrong? Why? Write your answer.

23 Look at the picture on page 25. What do you see? And what do you know about the cat? Write about it

24 Do you feel sorry for Walter Burge? Why (not)?

25 It is a year later. Write a letter from Aunt Min to Claire. What has happened at the castle? Does Walter Burge talk to people now? Do people think he's crazy now or not?

26 Do you enjoy ghost stories? Why (not)? Write and say.

WORD LIST *with example sentences*

ago (adv) Today is Wednesday. Monday was two days *ago*.

burn (v) Put the paper in the fire and *burn* it.

castle (n) The walls of the *castle* were two metres thick.

coloured (adj) She had an orange-*coloured* hat.

cottage (n) In the village, there was one big house and about thirty *cottages*.

crazy (adj) He has strange ideas and does strange things. He's *crazy*.

ever (adv) Do you *ever* go there? No, I never go there.

far (adj, adv) It's not *far* from here – only about a kilometre.

field (n) There are some horses in this *field*.

footprints (n) We followed the animal's *footprints* in the snow.

ghost (n) Some people think there's a *ghost* in that old building.

mile (n) One *mile* = 1.6 kilometres.

must (v) We haven't got any food. We *must* go to the shops.

secret (n) Don't tell anybody. It's a *secret*.

servant (n) Rich people had a lot of *servants* in their homes in the old days.

soon (adv) Today is 29th January. It will be February *soon*.

stone (n) There are big *stones* and small stones in this old wall.

tower (n) It's a big old building with four tall *towers*.

witch (n) In old stories, *witches* are bad ugly old women.

worry (v) I'm OK. Don't *worry* about me.

Her baby is ill and she is very *worried*.

Three Short Stories of Sherlock Holmes
Sir Arthur Conan Doyle

Sherlock Holmes is a very clever man. When people have strange, difficult problems, they come to him. Where is Mr Hosmer Angel? Which student saw the exam paper before the exam? Why is somebody following Miss Smith? Can you find the answers before Sherlock Holmes does?

Pirates of the Caribbean
The Curse of the Black Pearl

Elizabeth lives on a Caribbean island, a very dangerous place. A young blacksmith is interested in her, but pirates are interested too. Where do the pirates come from and what do they want? Is there really a curse on their ship? And why can't they enjoy their gold?

Treasure Island
Robert Louis Stevenson

Young Jim Hawkins lives quietly by the sea with his mother and father. One day, Billy Bones comes to live with them and everything changes. Jim meets Long John Silver and they travel the seas to find Treasure Island.

There are hundreds of Penguin Readers to choose from – world classics, film adaptations, modern-day crime and adventure, short stories, biographies, American classics, non-fiction, plays ...

For a complete list of all Penguin Readers titles, please contact your local Pearson Longman office or visit our website.

www.penguinreaders.com

The Mummy

"Imhotep is half-dead and will be half-dead for all time."

The Mummy is an exciting movie. Imhotep dies in Ancient Egypt. 3,700 years later Rick O'Connell finds him. Imhotep is very dangerous. Can O'Connell send him back to the dead?

The Last of the Mohicans
James Fenimore Cooper

Uncas is the last of the Mohican Indians. He is with his father and Hawkeye when they meet Heyward. Heyward is taking the two young daughters of a British colonel to their father. But a Huron Indian who hates the British is near. Will the girls see their father again?

Robin Hood

Robin Hood robbed rich people and gave the money to the poor. He fought against the greedy Sheriff of Nottingham and bad Prince John and defended the beautiful Lady Marian. *Robin Hood is a folk-hero and the story is supposed to be true!*

The Prince and the Pauper
Mark Twain

Two babies are born on the same day in England. One boy is a prince and the other boy is from a very poor family. Ten years later, they change places for a game. But then the old king dies and they cannot change back. Will the poor boy be the new King of England?

Robinson Crusoe
Daniel Defoe

Robinson Crusoe is shipwrecked onto an island after a storm at sea. Are there other people? How will he survive? Will he be rescued? *A classic tale of survival based on a true story.*

The Whistle and Dead Men's Eyes
M. R. James

Two Englishmen go away for a quiet holiday. But it is not very quiet in one man's hotel room. Somebody – or something – is using the other bed. What is it and why is it angry? The other man sees things, but they are not really there. Or are they? What is happening? Read these ghost stories and be afraid. Be very afraid!

Of Mice and Men
John Steinbeck

George and Lennie are friends and they have plans for the future. But Lennie is not very smart and he sometimes makes trouble. George wants to help him but that is not always easy. Then one night, when Lennie is alone, something happens. What can George do now? Can he help – or is it too late?

White Fang
Jack London

White Fang is a wolf from the mountains of Canada. His life is hard but he is happy in his world. Then he is taken to the world of men. There he learns to fight and to kill. White Fang knows nothing about love. But one day he meets Scott...

Fly Away Home
Patricia Hermes

Amy Alden finds a nest of Goose's eggs. The baby geese follow her all the time – they think she is her mother. Now the geese must fly south for the winter. Amy and her dad must help them fly away home...

There are hundreds of Penguin Readers to choose from – world classics, film adaptations, modern-day crime and adventure, short stories, biographies, American classics, non-fiction, plays ...

For a complete list of all Penguin Readers titles, please contact your local Pearson Longman office or visit our website.

Longman Dictionaries

Express yourself with confidence!

Longman has led the way in ELT dictionaries since 1935. We constantly talk to students and teachers around the world to find out what they need from a learner's dictionary.

Why choose a Longman dictionary?

Easy to understand

Longman invented the Defining Vocabulary – 2000 of the most common words which are used to write the definitions in our dictionaries. So Longman definitions are always clear and easy to understand.

Real, natural English

All Longman dictionaries contain natural examples taken from real-life that help explain the meaning of a word and show you how to use it in context.

Avoid common mistakes

Longman dictionaries are written specially for learners, and we make sure that you get all the help you need to avoid common mistakes. We analyse typical learners' mistakes and include notes on how to avoid them.

Innovative CD-ROMs

Longman are leaders in dictionary CD-ROM innovation. Did you know that a dictionary CD-ROM includes features to help improve your pronunciation, help you practice for exams and improve your writing skills?

For details of all Longman dictionaries, and to choose the one that's right for you, visit our website:

www.longman.com/dictionaries